XULON PRESS

The Saddest Little Hound Named Peter

Apostle L'Tanya C. Perry, MDiv

Illustrated By: Saad Ejaz

Xulon Press
2301 Lucien Way #415
Maitland, FL 32751
407.339.4217
www.xulonpress.com

© 2021 by Apostle L'Tanya C. Perry
Illustrations by Saad Ejaz

First printing edition 2021.

L'Tanya Perry
pastorperry@nbwcgf.org

www.ltanyaperry.org
www.mytap.org

Library of Congress Control Number: 2021912471

Paperback ISBN-13: 978-1-6628-2584-2
Hard Cover ISBN-13: 978-1-6628-2842-3
Ebook ISBN-13: 978-1-6628-2585-9

Dedication

There are times in our lives when we are in situations where we have to choose to stand for our faith in Jesus Christ, our Lord and Savior. This stand for our faith is accomplished verbally as well as by modeling the Word of God. Modeling Godly behavior is the best teacher.

I dedicate this book to my teacher, my mom, Essie Mae McCorkle. You truly adhered to Proverbs 22:6, "Train up a child in the way he should go, and when he is old, he will not depart from it." I'm a product of your modeling teaching of the Word of God! I try my best to model it in front of my children. Alexus and KJ, always remember Proverbs 22:6 and everything mom taught you!

Finally, I dedicate this book to my husband, Kelvin Perry, Sr.; thank you for allowing me to follow my God-given dreams. I love you dearly! Blue, my grand-dog! Thank you for your early morning prayer time with me. I know you are thankful for Kelvin being the dog whisperer to help you be the best grand-dog ever! He is your light beam whenever he gives you treats and high fives!

Happy Reading!

There lives a sad little hound.
He likes it better when no
one's around.

His name is Peter,
and his face is long.
He tells people he doesn't
believe in God, even though
he knows he's wrong.

When someone asks
if Peter believes in God,
he says, "No!"
But deep down,
Peter has faith.
It's just all a show!

Peter is sad
most days, you see.
He thinks he annoys
everyone around him,
kind of like a flea.

Peter denies his Lord
because most days
he feels sad.
And usually, he just
makes everyone
around him feel bad.

Peter loved to play
and run.
But now, the things
he used to like
no longer seem fun.

13

Peter just wants to
sleep and close his eyes.
When he's awake,
he just cries and cries.

Until one day,
this little hound had a dream.
A man appeared to him
like a beautiful light beam.

"You have denied me, but, I forgive you. Starting tomorrow, you will no longer feel blue."

"Tomorrow, you will have faith and believe.
And from here on out, you will be relieved!"

The next morning
Peter arises.
He doesn't feel sad;
he wants to
give out surprises.

Peter decides to go
on a nice long walk.
He sees some friends,
and they shout,
"Can we talk?"

"Sure," Peter says,
nodding his head.
And for the first time,
talking to people
didn't fill Peter with dread.

"Do you believe in God?"
Peter's friend wonders.
"I do!" Peter shouts,
and then they
hug one another.

Peter then goes for a run,
and he feels his best.
And from then on out,
Peter knew he was blessed!

About The Author

APOSTLE L'TANYA PERRY is a dynamic and proficient leader of our generation. In conjunction with a drive to influence God's people, her love for humanity has given birth to multiple books, one of which is this beautiful children's book. She's passionate about telling children's stories with illustrative images to help them learn with ease. For additional resources, visit our websites **ltanyaperry.org** or **mytap.org**, or subscribe to our *Facebook group: TAP.*

CPSIA information can be obtained
at www.ICGtesting.com
Printed in the USA
LVHW072103290921
699034LV00004B/102